THiS BOOK
BELONGS TO:

....

....

READ iT, LOVE iT,
AND PLEASE
RETURN iT

to all the children
SARAH

to the ghost
in the lift
LUCIA

little bee books

251 Park Avenue South, New York, NY 10010
Text copyright © 2020 by Sarah S. Brannen
Illustrations copyright © 2020 by Lucia Soto
Manufactured in China TPL 0420
First Edition

10 9 8 7 6 5 4 3 2 1

Library of Congress Cataloging-in-Publication Data
Names: Brannen, Sarah S., author. | Soto, Lucia, illustrator.
Title: Uncle Bobby's wedding / Sarah S. Brannen, Lucia Soto.
Description: New York, NY: Little Bee Books, [2020] | Originally published: New York: G. P. Putnam's Sons, 2008.
Audience: Ages 3–6. | Audience: Grades K–1. | Summary: Chloe is jealous and sad when her favorite uncle announces
that he will be getting married, but as she gets to know Jamie better and becomes involved in planning the wedding,
she discovers that she will always be special to Uncle Bobby—and to Uncle Jamie, too. | Identifiers: LCCN 2019041949
Subjects: CYAC: Uncles—Fiction. | Weddings—Fiction. | Same-sex marriage—Fiction. | Gays—Fiction. | Classification: LCC
PZ7.B737514 Unc 2020 | DDC [E]—dc23 LC record available at https://lccn.loc.gov/2019041949
ISBN 978-1-4998-1008-0
littlebeebooks.com

For more information about special discounts on bulk purchases,
please contact Little Bee Books at sales@littlebeebooks.com.

UNCLE BOBBY'S WEDDING

words SARAH S. BRANNEN

pictures LUCIA SOTO

Bobby was Chloe's favorite uncle.

He took her rowing on the river.
He taught her the names of the stars.

Once, they even climbed to
the top of a lighthouse.
"Let's live here!" said Chloe.
"I'd like that," said Uncle Bobby.

Most of all, Chloe loved flying kites with Uncle Bobby. So when Mama planned the first picnic of summer, Chloe was as happy as a ladybug.

Mama and Chloe made sun tea and fried chicken, corn bread and rhubarb pie. Bobby and his friend, Jamie, brought bottles of fizzy cider.

After pie, Uncle Bobby and Jamie made an announcement. "We're getting married!" said Uncle Bobby.

Mama whooped and hugged him. Daddy shook hands with Jamie. Everyone was smiling and talking and crying and laughing.

Everyone except . . . Chloe.

"Mama," said Chloe, "I don't understand! Why is Uncle Bobby getting married?"
"Bobby and Jamie love each other," said Mama. "When grown-up people love each other that much, sometimes they get married."

"But," said Chloe, "Bobby is my special uncle.
I don't want him to get married."
"I think you should talk to him," said Mama.

Chloe found Uncle Bobby sitting on a swing.
"Why do you have to get married?" she asked.
"Jamie and I want to live together and have
our own family," said Bobby.

"You want kids?"
"Only if they're just like you," said Bobby.

"That's a pretty good reason," said Chloe.

"But—" said Chloe.
"But what?" asked Uncle Bobby.
"But I still don't think you should get married.
I want us to keep having fun together like always."

"I promise we'll still have fun together," said Bobby.
"You'll always be my sweet pea."

Bobby and Jamie asked Chloe to go to the ballet with them.

Afterward, they had ice cream sodas.

Jamie imitated the ballet dancers and Chloe laughed
so hard, she got soda up her nose.

Uncle Bobby and Jamie taught Chloe to sail. She fell in the water at the dock, but Jamie dove in after her.

Then Bobby jumped in, too, and they all swam until suppertime.

At night, Chloe, Bobby, and Jamie sang songs
by the campfire and toasted marshmallows.

"I wish both of you were my uncles," said Chloe.

"Well, you're getting your wish," said Jamie.
"When we get married, I'll be your uncle, too."

On the day of the wedding,
Chloe put on her new dress.

Everyone was excited and busy.

Uncle Bobby lost the rings.

Jamie couldn't tie his bow tie.

Chloe found the rings in Bobby's jacket pocket. She helped Jamie with his tie. And she helped Mama put the perfect finishing touches on the wedding cake. "We're ready!" said Chloe.

An afternoon breeze cooled the garden. Daisies and violets bloomed in the grass and the air smelled like roses. Cousins, grandparents, and friends watched Chloe walk down the aisle holding a basket of flowers.

She was so happy, she felt like doing a cartwheel. Instead, she scattered flower petals all around.

And then Bobby and Jamie got married.

"That was the best wedding ever!" said Chloe.
"I think so, too," said Uncle Jamie.

The band started to play. Chloe jumped up and grabbed Uncle Bobby's and Uncle Jamie's hands.